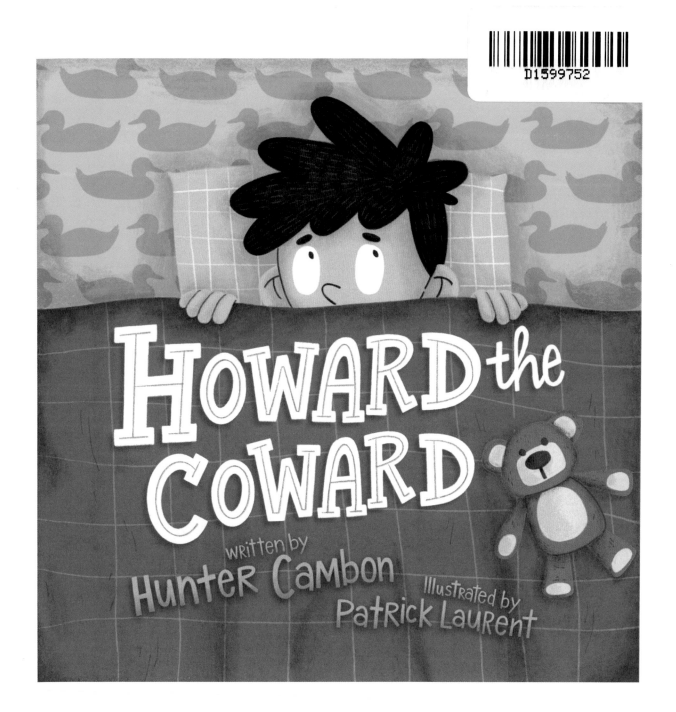

HOWARD the COWARD

written by
Hunter Cambon

Illustrated by
Patrick Laurent

INSPIREBYTES OMNI MEDIA

Howard the Coward

ISBN Paperback: 978-1-953445-38-4
ISBN E-book: 978-1-953445-44-5

Library of Congress Control Number: 2023940713

This book was responsibly printed using print-on-demand technology in order to minimize its impact on the planet and the environment. Learn more at:
www.inspirebytes.com/why-we-publish-differently/

▌ INSPIREBYTES OMNI MEDIA

Inspirebytes Omni Media LLC
PO Box 988
Wilmette, IL 60091

For more information, please visit www.inspirebytes.com.

For kids with fears (both realized and not).
Things aren't as scary as they seem.
Keep taking the next step!

And for Kimberly, Laudy, Mom & Dad:
Thanks for helping me learn this lesson myself.

Readers: Can you find all of the ducks around Howard's home?

Howard the Coward lies shaking in his bed
while he shivers and quivers with covers overhead.
He's thirsty for water. His throat feels so dry.
If he doesn't get some soon, he thinks he might die.

1

Howard has this problem
almost every night
because he crawls into bed
without water in sight.

2

He tries to remember,
but he didn't tonight.
So here he is again,
stuck in this plight.

3

"I MUST GET SOME WATER!"

Howard then thinks.
But the darkness that surrounds him
makes his heart sink.

The fear and panic are making him fret,
but his thirst is something he cannot forget.

He makes his way
out of his room to the hall.
His thirst begins calling,
and he must answer the call.

6

He keeps his eyes open
for what he might see;
peering into the darkness—
what could there be?

He hears something creak
at the foot of the stairs.
What is that sound
that gives him this scare?

Should he check? Should he look?
Should he see? Does he dare?

Phew!

It's only a screen, an old rusty screen.
One that could use a wash, and maybe a clean.

CLICK

He continues to creep
down the steps through the hall.
He's so scared and barely moving,
he basically crawls.

What is that sound
that sounds like a scream?
Is it some scary creature
scheming a scheme?

11

No, it's a twig scratching his window, you see.
It's the sound that is made by the wind in the trees.

All of these sounds that are making him quake
make him want to check things out, for his family's sake.
Howard pushes on to see what may loom,
thinking this could be the start of his doom.

OooooooooO!

CREAK! SLINK!

EEEEK!

WHOOSH!

BANG!

CRASH!

14

He peeks down the stairs
and creeps down the hall,
but something makes him stop,
and it doesn't sound small.

15

Howard is right; it really isn't small.
It's the air conditioning unit and not scary at all.

Calming himself down, he continues ahead,
but immediately wishes he were back in his bed.
For something below lets out a small cry,
making Howard jump as high as the sky.

As Howard looks around
and behind all the doors,
he realizes what it is—
the old wooden floors.

18

Now into the dining room
without making a peep,
Howard keeps quiet.
He should be asleep.

19

**CREAK!
CRACK!**

What is that creak, that crack? Should he hide?

Nope, it's the dog rolling back on her side.

He pets his pet
but grows scared to the core
knowing he must check
behind the foyer door.

There in the corner
stands a man tall and still!
His heart begins to race,
giving Howard a thrill.

23

He keeps moving forward, now on his toes,
but realizes the "man" is a coat rack wearing Dad's clothes.

24

So Howard keeps moving,
checking things are okay,
when he sees something
outside beginning to sway.

He creeps to the window, trying to keep cool,
only to find the breeze brushing over the pool.

With his thirst taking over (he so needs a drink),
but how to get water, Howard still thinks.
Should he jump, or run, or skip, or dash?
All of these ways could get him there fast.

Howard decides to skate his way through
while lying on his belly—he thinks this will do.

Now into to the kitchen,
Howard the Coward must head
before being able
to return to his bed.
But on his way in,
on his skateboard he flies,
something overhead
waits in surprise!
It makes awful sounds!
A gasp and a scream!
This is the end!
Or so it may seem.

As he rolls closer
and with a face full of fear,
he wishes he had a sword,
a shield, or a spear.

31

But to his surprise
and with a look of disbelief,
he sees it's an old ceiling fan
and sighs with relief.

Howard the Coward made it! The kitchen is his!
His biggest fears conquered, at least for now, that is.
As he pours his glass of water, quenching his crave,
He says to himself,

"Wow! I'm HOWARD the BRAVE!"

Sipping his water
and enjoying the glory,
he chuckles and thinks,
"This'll make a good story."
Howard feels silly
for once being so afraid
and whispers once more,
"I'm Howard the Brave."

So through the house he walks without a fear in his head
feeling happy and safe to return to his bed.

He turns off the fan as he glances at his pool
and thinks he'll go swimming tomorrow after school.

He brushes off dad's coat and scratches his dog's belly
while slipping her a snack, some meat from the deli.

His steps are quite sure
now that the floors are not scary
while grabbing more blankets
than he thinks he can carry.

39

He makes himself comfortable,
comfy blankets in a heap
with the trees and the wind
to help lull him to sleep.

As he drifts into dreams
while lying in bed,
he feels proud to know
there is nothing to dread.

40

He overcame his fear
and the road is now paved,
not for Howard the Coward, but for

HOWARD
the BRAVE.

About the Author

Hunter Cambon is a Florida native who enjoys pursuing seaside passions and spending time with friends and family. He likes to write and create, drawing inspiration from his surroundings. His interests led him to teach literature for the majority of his career, sharing his gifts and strengths with young minds.

When Hunter is not writing, working, or enjoying the outdoors, he loves adventuring with his wife and dog overseas and in the United States. *Howard the Coward* is Hunter's first children's book.

Learn more about Hunter at howardthecoward.com

About the Illustrator

Patrick Laurent is the creative artist behind Laurent Collective. He began his career in art when he was in elementary school, drawing and creating sports characters and selling them to his friends. He has gone on to create a body of work that can be found in homes across the globe through art prints, apparel, homeware, and books.

Patrick is from Indiana and now lives and works in London with his family. His aim is to create work that reminds everyone that they have something unique to offer the world.

Learn more about Patrick at laurentcollective.com

41696672R00031